The Ghost of Parkview Ranch

Nicole Simon

Published by Nicole Simon, 2024.

THE GHOST OF PARKVIEW RANCH

First edition. February 1, 2024.

Copyright © 2024 Nicole Simon.

ISBN: 979-8224476930

Written by Nicole Simon.

The Ghost of Parkview Ranch

A Cowboy Love Story

1

Nicole Simon

© Copyright 2023 - All rights reserved.

Chapter 1: Tragedy

Melissa pulls back the curtains in her bedroom and opens them wide to see what the day looks like. It is still dark outside, but dawn has always been her favorite time of day. She always gets up right before the sun is getting ready to rise and makes herself some coffee to sip while she sits on the porch and watches the sunrise. Once that is finished, she gets started on her daily chores at her family's ranch.

It was the same routine every day, but she had never gotten tired of it so far. As she sits outside on the front porch, she sips her coffee and smiles as the sky begins its morning display of warm red and orange swirls painted across the Montana sky. She smiles as she finishes her coffee and sets the mug back in the kitchen before making her way to the stables.

The moment her foot breaches the entrance, her horse, Dusky, begins excitingly whinnying and trotting in place. Melissa walks over to him and places her hand gently on his snout. "Hey, boy," she says before kissing his forehead. "Are you ready to go riding today?"

Dusky neighs in response, and Melissa laughs as she readjusts her light blue cowboy hat before opening the stall and stepping inside to get him ready. It takes her a few minutes to get everything prepared and to secure the saddle and reins, and by the time she is finished, she and Dusky are both eager to get moving.

Melissa leads her horse out of the stables and finds her brother Mark standing there. "Good morning," she chirps. "Do you have a lot to do today? If you don't, I was thinking maybe we could go for a ride together later."

"I'll need to get back to you on that," he replies. "I want to, but Dad says there are a lot of things that need to get done today since he is going out of town soon."

"Oh, yeah. I forgot he has that meeting this week about the chickens. Do you think he is actually considering getting them?"

"I certainly hope so," Mark says with a laugh. "Some fresh eggs would really be nice. I wouldn't even mind caring for them as long as I got some free eggs out of it."

Melissa laughs. "Okay, well, if you change your mind, just come find me." She waves at him before turning and starting to head toward the paddock. Unlatching the gate, she leads Dusky inside before shutting it behind her. Once they are both inside, she hoists herself into the saddle and nudges Dusky to start walking. "You know, today is the day I plan to take you onto the trail, right?" she asks, rubbing his ear. "We just need to make sure you're ready to go first."

She kicks his sides gently, and he begins trotting around the paddock gracefully. Melissa has always loved riding her horse, and she can't remember a time when it wasn't the first thing she'd done in the morning. Even after 34 years, she has never grown tired of caring for her horses. She can't remember a time in her life when she wasn't caring for them, and she still loves it.

After a few minutes of trotting around to let Dusky get warmed up, she dismounts and walks over to the gate. As she reaches for the latch, her father walks up to her and signals for her to wait. He looks out of breath, and Melissa frowns. "Is something wrong?"

He shakes his head. "No, but your mother would like to see you, and I wanted to catch you before you and Dusky took off."

"Oh, well, thank you for letting me know," she says before glancing back at Dusky. "Would you be willing to stay with him while I talk to Mom?"

He nods. "I would be happy too. Just try not to take too long because I have to be getting going soon myself."

Melissa smiles and hands him the reins. "Thank you," she says before heading back toward the house. When she steps inside, she can smell fresh bacon being cooked along with whatever else her mother came up with for breakfast.

When Melissa walks in, her mother is standing over the stove, stirring a pot, and she seems completely focused. "I was told you wanted to see me?"

At the sound of her voice, Melissa's mother turns around to face her. "Yes, I'm glad I caught you before you left. There is something I was hoping to speak with you about."

Melissa's mouth goes dry as she listens to her mother. She knows just as well as anyone that it is hardly a good thing if her mother wants to speak about something. "What's wrong?" she questions cautiously.

"I know you have plans, but I realized this morning that we are out of potatoes, and I will need those to make dinner. If you wouldn't mind stopping by the store on your way home to grab some things, I would greatly appreciate it."

A wave of relief washes over Melissa as she realizes she's not in trouble. "Sure, I can do that," she replies. "I don't plan on being out too long, so I can bring them with me on my way home."

Her mother smiles warmly. "Thank you," she says before reaching into her apron, pulling out a few bills, and handing them to Melissa, who takes them and carefully slips them into her back pocket.

"I'll be back soon." Melissa kisses her mother on the cheek before turning and making her way out of the house and back to Dusky.

By the time she returns to her father and Dusky, a wide smile is spread across her face. "Look at that. Dusky loves you already," she says with a light chuckle. "All that said, Mother would like me to stop and get a few things on the way home, so I may be out a little longer than expected."

"Are you sure you don't want to bring anyone with you?" he asks. "I worry about you when you go off on your own."

Melissa shakes her head. "I'll be fine. Besides, I have Dusky with me to keep me safe."

He smiles as he dismounts the horse and hands her the reins. "Okay, as long as you're safe, I'm okay with it." He turns to look at Dusky. "Remember, it's your job to take care of her," he tells the horse.

She laughs in response before mounting Dusky and double-checking to ensure she has everything she needs. "I love you," she says to her father as he opens the gate so she can raise her horse out of the paddock.

"I love you too," her father replies as he latches the gate closed behind him.

Without wasting any more time, Melissa takes off down the trail. It has been a long time since she went on a ride like this. Her favorite feeling is the breeze flowing through her hair as she breathes in the fresh air. As they continue down the trail, the grass gets a little longer. Since no one owns the neighboring property, the yard tends to get out of control.

Thankfully, it isn't a long walk to get through. She remembers the first time she rode down the path and smiles. Things had been different when she was a child, and looking back on it, she finds herself grateful for all the experiences she's had.

Melissa is lost in her thoughts as Dusky moves through the tall grass. When the horse comes to a sudden stop, she is broken from her thoughts. "Whoa, what's the matter, boy?" she asks as she strokes his neck to try and comfort him. The horse seems to calm down for a moment, but as soon as Melissa lets go of the harness, Dusky neighs loudly and rears back on his hind legs before smashing his hooves back into the ground with force.

Fear begins to seep into Melissa's chest as she holds on tight to try and keep from falling off the horse. She hears a quiet rattling sound coming from beneath them and realizes a rattlesnake must be nearby. She places her hand on Dusky again, only for him to start bucking frantically, trying to escape the snake.

Melissa does her best to hold on, but it isn't enough. In his panic, Dusky throws her from his back and onto the ground. When she lands, her head smashes into a rock, immediately knocking her unconscious.

***

When Melissa finally opens her eyes, she finds herself floating above her own body. She tries to reach out with her trembling hands to move back into her body, but it doesn't work. Breathing is hard, and before she knows it, an ambulance pulls in and at least four people jump out of the back and begin tending to her. She has no idea how they found her or even who they are, which she finds unsettling.

She stares down at her own body as the EMTs work on her and do their best to revive her. *Is this really how my life is going to end?* She asks herself. *I don't want to die yet. There are so many things I still need to do with my life. What about Dusky? Was he bit by the snake?* All these questions and dozens more fill her mind, only causing her to panic more.

Just this morning, she had been happy and ready to start the day, and now she's worried she will never see the light of day again. For all she knows, she is dead, and there is nothing the paramedics can do to help her. The thought makes her stomach turn, and she closes her eyes.

Eventually, one of the EMTs manages to get a pulse, and the next thing she knows, her body is being loaded up into the ambulance. Since the ranch is a good distance from town, the paramedics explain that they want to get her moved as soon as possible so she can get better care.

Melissa has no clue what to think about any of it, and once she makes it to the hospital, she learns that her body has entered into a coma. If she still had her body there, Melissa is sure she would have already broken down in tears. All she wants is to wake up and go back to how things were. She was happy, and now it's as though everything is being torn away from her.

What hurts the most is the realization that she cannot speak or interact with anyone. She is convinced they can't even see her, which only makes her feel worse. *Why did this happen to me? Am I going to die? Did something happen to Dusky?*

The same questions run through her head repeatedly as she struggles to process what is happening. She struggles to remember why she is here but her memories are nothing but a blur. Her mother and father sit on each side of her, each holding one of her hands.

"We love you more than you will ever know," her mother says before gently kissing her hand. "I'm so sorry this happened to you."

Before anyone else can speak up, the doctor steps into the room. "Hello, Mr. and Mrs. Anderson. Thankfully, we were able to keep your daughter stable long enough to get her here. Unfortunately, her injuries are pretty severe. She's entered into a coma, and we don't know how long it will be before she wakes up. There is a chance she won't ever wake up. We are doing the best we can, but at this time, I can promise nothing."

Melissa sees her parents' hearts shatter as they receive the news. However, she just feels numb. She has no idea how any of this is even possible and wishes she could find a way to speak with her parents. *They need to know I'm still alive,* she thinks to herself. Unfortunately, she has no way to prove it, and as far as she can tell, it could be a long time before she can leave the hospital.

Chapter 2: Alone

Melissa's parents visit her every day in the hospital, but no matter how hard she tries to communicate with them, they never hear her. Her mother holds her hand and cries as she apologizes over and over again. Since the accident, her mother has blamed herself. Melissa wants to tell her mom the truth and let her know everything is okay, but since there is no way for her mother to see her, all her efforts are in vain.

"You need to stop blaming yourself, love," her father says as he places a hand on his wife's shoulder. "What happened was a terrible accident, but we raised a strong daughter, and there is no doubt in my mind that she will pull through this."

Her mother shakes her head. "I know our daughter is strong, but this would have never happened had I not sent her into town."

"Emily, my love, she would have gone out riding whether you sent her or not. Blaming yourself isn't going to help her. Just talk to her. I've heard that sometimes people in a coma can hear everything happening around them. That means you can still talk to her even though she can't respond."

If only they knew just how true that is, Melissa thinks. It hurts to know nothing she does will help her mother. Being able to see her and hear her, but not touch her or speak with her is heart-wrenching. Melissa has always been close to her parents, and she feels lost without being able to talk to them now.

Her mother looks down at Melissa as she lies unconscious in her hospital bed. She is hooked up to several machines, and there are tubes and wires all over the place. Even her face is covered with a ventilator. She remembers the nurses saying something about her being unable to breathe on her own, which scared her, but for some reason, it's the only thing she can think about now.

She wonders if this is how she's going to die and wishes more than anything that she could tell her parents what happened. Melissa can feel her mother's heartbreak like a physical weight on her chest as her parents start to pack up their things to leave for the day. She doesn't want them to leave but knows she can do nothing to make them stay.

Once they are gone, Melissa sits in the chair beside her body and watches her chest rise and fall with each breath. She doesn't understand how anything she is experiencing is possible. Melissa had never been one to believe in ghosts, yet here she is, floating around while the rest of her family cry about her. Being able to see herself from the outside is a strange feeling. No matter what she does, there is nothing she can do to change anything. It isn't like the movies. Instead of feeling free to do as she wishes, she feels lost and alone. However, as she sits there, an idea pops into her mind.

Wait, I wonder if I can head back home. I've never tried leaving this place, so maybe all I need to do is walk home. Without my body, it should make this a lot easier, right?

Melissa shakes her head, feeling completely insane. Part of her wonders if this is all just a terrible dream that she's on the brink of waking up from, but something tells her that isn't the case.

Taking one last look at her body, Melissa turns and steps out of the hospital room. She halfway expects nurses to come rushing over to ask if she is okay, only to remember that no one can see her. She walks out of the hospital without any trouble and manages to find a way home. It takes her a few hours to get there, though by the time she arrives, a wave of relief washes over her. Being home after everything that happened feels better than she can describe, though it still hurts to know there is nothing she can do to help her family feel better.

Melissa makes her way into the house and looks around. Everything looks the same, just a little more cluttered than usual. Everyone in the home seems sad and distracted, and guilt begins to pulse through her. While no one blames her for what happened, she feels like she's abandoned her family.

There has to be some way to show them I'm still here, she thinks as she looks around the room. As her eyes land on the living room, she sees her mother sitting there with a book, though she isn't sure if she is actually reading it or not. Beside her is a picture of Melissa in her prom dress. Even though it feels like a lifetime ago, her mother loves the picture and said she would keep it there forever.

The memory makes her smile as an idea pops into her head. Using her spirit, Melissa inches closer to the picture and attempts to knock it to the ground. Her fingers go right through it the first few times, and she starts to wonder if moving things around is even possible or if it is just something seen in the movies.

Doing her best to focus on the picture frame, she tries again and, this time knocks it to the floor. Her mother sits up, startled, and looks down at the picture. Fresh tears well in her eyes as she picks it up without much thought. Melissa frowns when she realizes her mother believes the picture fell on its own.

"Mom, I'm right here. You don't need to worry about me. I will find a way back to you, I promise."

Unfortunately, her words fall on deaf ears. More shame and guilt pulse through her. She wants things to go back to how they were but is starting to wonder if her body is ever going to wake up. Melissa stands there watching her mother for several minutes before finally returning to the hospital. Knowing her mother can't hear her or see her is too painful.

Over the next two weeks, Melissa finds herself doing all she can to gain her mother and father's attention so they know she is still there. Every time they talk about her, she uses gusts of wind to blow open the windows and knock down any pictures of herself. Her parents would notice, but they would never put it together. They just assume they need to fix the windows or secure the pictures.

Before she knows it, an entire month has already gone by. Still unable to connect with her family, Melissa wonders if she will ever wake up from her coma. Every day she sees herself lying there and wills herself to wake up but to no avail. Nothing she does works, and having no one to talk to is torture.

When she returns to the ranch one night, she sees that her father has hired a new worker to care for the horses. His name is Richard. He is about 40 years old, with dark hair that gives him a rugged look. Melissa catches herself staring at the handsome cowboy when she first meets him and eventually realizes he is there to care for her horse.

Taking care of Dusky has always been her favorite part of the day, and it hurts her to know there is nothing she can do for him as long as she's in a coma. She never blames Dusky for what happened and is just grateful her horse is okay and that he managed to avoid the snake.

After about a week, Melissa finds herself watching Richard and Dusky every day. They spend a lot of time together, and Melissa enjoys seeing how well he treats her horse.

"Hey, buddy," he says as he walks into the stables at 7 a.m.—the same time he comes in every evening. "Today, we are going to go for a ride. How would you like that?"

Dusky neighs with excitement. "That's what I want to hear," says Richard with a smile on his face. "Let me just gather up your things, and we can get this show on the road." He steps out of the stall and gathers everything he needs before returning to Dusky. It doesn't take him very long to get him saddled up, and within minutes he is already walking out of the stable with Dusky right beside him.

Melissa is sitting on the fence with a smile on her face. Since she cannot connect with others, she finds this to be the most peaceful time of day. While Richard has no idea she's there, she is confident that Dusky knows. Richard is getting ready to mount Dusky when his eyes lock on the part of the fence where Melissa is sitting.

If she didn't know better, she would swear he was looking right at her. As he steps closer, his eyes widen, and he reaches out toward her. She believes he will touch her for a moment and feels a jolt of anxiety before she disappears, only to reappear back in the hospital. Confusion takes over as she stares at her spirit, wondering what happened and how it was even possible. Ever since her accident, she had walked back to the ranch every day, but this time, it is like she teleported.

She tries to appear back at the ranch, but nothing happens. Regardless, it still excites her. Even though she is only a spirit, she feels more alive than she has in years. Something about the way Richard looked at her made her feel strange. He is a kind and hardworking man with a good heart—or, at least, that is what she keeps telling herself. The way he acts with Dusky warms her heart, and she knew from the moment she met him that he's special.

Whenever she thinks about him, she pictures his hand reaching her. While she knows he likely didn't actually see her, she likes to pretend he did. His simply getting close to her is the most contact she's had in a long time. As she looks over at her body, she frowns. Her body is still hooked up to machines, and as far as she can tell, it doesn't look like she will be waking anytime soon.

Gathering her confidence, Melissa heads back to the ranch to see if she can find Richard again. By the time she gets there, the sun has completely set, taking away most of her light. She looks around for Richard, but he is nowhere to be seen. When she doesn't see him, she makes her way into the stables to find Dusky standing there asleep.

A smile appears on her face as she watches him. Being around him always made her feel good; even now, as just a spirit, that remains the same. She has bonded with her horse since day one, which is also why she could never be angry about what happened. Since Richard is nowhere to be found, Melissa turns her gaze to the ground in disappointment. Even if he can't see or hear her, she still loves spending time with him and watching him as he works.

Deciding he must have gone home for the night, Melissa returns to the hospital. When she gets there, she is surprised to see her mother sitting there beside her holding her hand. "I know if you were here you would lecture me for being up so late," she says, her voice breaking just like it always does when she tries to say something upsetting.

"It's not too late!" Melissa shouts to deaf ears. "I'm right here, Mom. Please, listen to me! I—"

Her mother breaks down in tears as she gently squeezes her daughter's hand. The woman is clearly broken up by everything happening around her. Melissa has always looked up to her mother because of how hard she tries to ensure everyone is taken care of. She's never let anything get in her way, even if she was sick, working, or caring for children. Everything somehow always got done.

While Melissa never appreciated this as a child growing up on the ranch, now that she's older, she's beginning to realize that things don't always work out the way people want them to. Since she isn't sure if her body will wake up again, she wants to do all she can to help around the ranch.

Chapter 3: New Friends

Richard gazes toward the fence, wondering if the woman he'd seen would return. While it's possible it was nothing more than a trick of the eye, he doesn't want to believe that as truth. Something about the woman lit a fire inside him, leaving him desperate to learn more about her.

Dusky trots in place and nudges his shoulder. "Okay, okay. We can go for a ride," he says. "I know you're getting impatient." He reaches next to him, pulls a brush from his bag, and begins brushing Dusky. "Just a little bit longer. I want to make sure you're clean and well-groomed before taking you out."

He smiles as he finishes brushing Dusky and secures his harness and bridle. Right as he is about to mount the horse, his eyes move back to the fence, where he sees the woman from the other night sitting there. His eyes widen as he takes a few steps toward her, not wanting to look away for fear she will disappear. Dusky neighs excitedly behind him. "You see her too, don't you, buddy," he says, keeping his eyes locked on her. She's the most beautiful woman he's ever laid eyes on, and he opens his mouth to speak to her, but she disappears before he could get the words out.

Richard frowns, wondering why he can't get close to her. He can still see her face in his mind and wishes he knew more about her. While a small part of him believes he is just saying things, the other part wants to get to know her. Even though they have never met, something about her draws him in.

Seeing her disappear as soon as he gets close leaves him feeling disappointed. Trying to push the thought of her from his head, he mounts Dusky, and the two of them head out on their daily ride. By the time they return, the sun is high in the sky. He leads Dusky back to the stables before heading toward the house for a break and some fresh water.

When he enters the house, he sees Mark cooking something. "Hey," he says when he notices Richard walk in. "Do you want me to make you something too?"

"That would be great," he replies before taking a seat. "I actually have something I want to talk to you about."

Mark glances over at him, raising his brow. "Oh? What might that be?"

"I know this may sound crazy, but as I was taking care of Dusky, I saw a picture of this woman," he says, choosing his words carefully so Mark won't think he's crazy. "I don't know if she lives here or anything, but I want to talk to her."

"You saw a picture?" he asks as he finishes plating the first plate and starts cracking more eggs into the pan. "What did she look like?"

Richard thinks about it momentarily, trying to remember every detail of her face. "She was slim with long dark hair. If I had to guess, I would say she was in her thirties. Her face—"

Before he can finish speaking, Mark abruptly stops what he's doing to open one of the drawers beside him and hand a photo to Richard. His mouth goes dry as he stares at it. Sure enough, he finds himself staring at the same face he'd seen earlier. "W-who is this?" he stutters.

"That's Melissa. She's my sister, and Dusky is her horse. Unfortunately, she was in a terrible accident. Dusky was startled and threw her from his back. Right now, she's in the hospital in a coma. Your description of the girl in the picture matched hers, so I figured she's who you saw. Was I right?"

Confusion swirls around in Richard's mind. *If the girl is in a coma, then why do I keep seeing her? We've never even met before, so there has to be something going on. Right?*

He isn't entirely sure what to make of the news and wonders if going back to her is the best move. On the one hand, he might have found the woman of his dreams, but on the other hand, he is starting to wonder if he's just going crazy. Pulling himself back to reality, Richard glances over at Mark and nods. "Yep, this is her," he replies. "You said she's in a coma? That's awful."

"Sure is. Our mom is taking it pretty hard and blames herself, but we all still have faith that she will wake up." After sliding his eggs off the pan and onto a plate, he turns off the stove. "Oh, and sorry you had to go through your first week solo. Brian should be back tomorrow, and he will help you with anything you don't understand."

Richard smiles. "No worries, this is all stuff I've done before. But I look forward to meeting Brian. Anyway, have a good night," he says, eager to get out of the house so he could have a moment with his thoughts.

Was I just seeing things? How could I have known what Melissa looked like when I'd never met her before?

He debates going to the hospital to see her in person, but he decides against it and chooses to just turn in for the night. Richard made his way to the bunkie set up for him by the house. It's not the biggest space, but it's enough. There's a tiny kitchenette in one corner and a bed in the other. The bathroom is attached to the back of the small setup, which Richard feels is more than sufficient to get him by until he is able to make renovations—he is thankful that the Andersons gave him the option to expand his small living area.

With Melissa still on his mind, Richard crawls into his bed and pulls the covers over him. With all the excitement of the day, he finds himself completely exhausted and manages to fall asleep within a matter of minutes.

***

The following morning, Richard is up early. The sun hasn't even begun to rise as he begins his new daily ritual. Once he is dressed, he brushes his teeth, pours some coffee into his thermos, and heads out to the stables. When he steps inside, he is surprised to see there is already a man a few years older than him standing there.

The man turns around and grins as he tips his cowboy hat in greeting. "You must be Richard. I was told you started yesterday and managed to get everything done on your own. That really is quite the feat, you know? Anyway," he says as he holds out his hand for Richard to shake. "My name is Brian. It's great to meet you."

Richard takes his hand and shakes it. "It's good to meet you too. I've been doing ranch work all my life, so it isn't very difficult to get the hang of things. Though, I'm sure there are some things you do differently here, so I would love to know the correct process."

Brian smiles. "You sound like just the type of person I want to work with. I've worked here for the past 20 years, so if there is something I do differently from everyone else, I would have no way of knowing what it is. As long as everything is taken care of, the how doesn't really matter to the Andersons. From what I can tell, you did a great job, even being alone for the whole week. Everything looks great, and I didn't have to fix anything, so you're already doing better than our previous ranch hand."

"Really?" asks Richard, tilting his head slightly. "What happened to the previous guy?"

"Nothing too bad. The kid was just full of himself and rarely helped us get anything done. Unless we told him exactly what to do, he would just stand there in the way all day."

"Oh, wow. I'm guessing he didn't last long?"

Brian laughed. "He was here for the entire damn winter last year. We finally let him go in the spring."

"That's good to know," Richard replies as he walks over to Dusky before glancing over at the fence. Since he isn't expecting to see her, when he turns his head, he is completely caught off guard. There she is, just like she was before. As much as he wants to walk over to her and strike up a conversation, he knows it isn't a good idea. The last thing he wants is for Brian to see her, so he swiftly moves his attention back to Dusky. "Once I'm done brushing this guy's coat, I'm planning on taking him out for a ride. Do you want to join us?"

Brian grins. "I think that's an excellent idea," he says as he begins caring for the horse in the stall beside Dusky's.

"Is that your horse?" Richard asks as he runs the brush through Dusky's mane.

Brian shakes his head. "No, this isn't my horse. Actually, my horse passed away a few months back. Since then, I've just been walking everywhere and getting rides where I can. I know I should get another horse, but I had my last horse for years, and I can't get another horse while still grieving."

"I can understand that," Richard says as he gets Dusky saddled up. "Taking care of these animals every day isn't what everyone thinks. We bond with them and get to know them. Caring for animals is a lot of work, and losing them is even harder. I really am sorry for your loss."

Brain smiles. "You don't need to be sorry. Crimson was always a good horse. He had a good, long, and full life, and he passed away in his sleep, so it wasn't painful. I'll get a new horse eventually, I just want to make sure I'm ready before taking the leap."

The two men lead their horses out of the stables before looking up at the sky. "Looks like we'll be getting some rain soon," Richard notes before glancing back at the fence. The woman, who looks like Melissa, seems to be staring right at him, though since he knows she is in a coma, he wonders if it's just his mind playing tricks on him. "Hey, do you see anything on that fence over there?" he asks, pointing right to where Melissa is sitting.

Brian looks around the area before shaking his head. "I don't see anything. Why? Did you see something?"

Not wanting to seem crazy, Richard shakes his head. "Nah. I thought I did, but it must have just been a reflection of something."

"If you say so. Just remember, since we are going to be working together as partners, that means you need to push yourself to do your best. It is clear to me that you're good at your job, so there is a chance you're going to be here for a very long time."

Richard smiles. "I hope to be here a long time. I love it here and I know I am more than capable of completing the work." He nods toward

Brian. "What about you? What got you into ranching? Is it something you grew up doing, or is it something you started when you were older?"

"Well," Brian says, recalling the memories. "I grew up on a ranch with my father. My mother died when I was born, so she was never around. As soon as I was old enough, I was doing everything my dad was. Unfortunately, he was forced to sell the ranch when he got sick. He did what he could to keep it, but ultimately, he could no longer afford it. That's when I got my job here." he says proudly.

"Wow, you must really like it here to have been here for so long."

"I do. Everyone here is great; whenever I need something, they are always there to help. Honestly, this place feels more like home than work. We all get along well, and we work hard to keep things running smoothly."

Richard smiles. "That sounds like exactly the type of place I would love working for. I've only been here for a day, but I truly love it so far."

The two men continue their talk as they ride their horses around the property before returning to the stables. Once Dusky is put inside, Richard smiles and looks at Brian. "Now we need to clean the place," he says, waving his hand in front of his nose.

As Richard pushes the wheelbarrow he had just filled with waste from the barn, he notices Melissa sitting on the fence again. He tries to approach her once more, but just like last time, she disappears before he can get too close.

Chapter 4: Finally Seen

Melissa looks down at her body as she lies in the hospital bed, looking no better than the day before. More than anything, she wants to go back to the way things were. Being trapped in a coma and traveling around as a ghost that no one can see or hear has her feeling like she's going insane.

She heads to the ranch daily and watches Richard as he works. She rarely sees him without Brian, and they are always laughing and talking to each other. Seeing the two cowboys get along so well brings a smile to her face, though she still wishes she could find a way to reach out to Richard. Whenever she sits on the fence to watch him, she always notices his eyes locked on her. Since no one else can see her, she assumes he can't either, though the fact that his eyes always linger on her makes her wonder if she truly is invisible to him.

It has been nearly a week since Richard started working at the ranch, and the more she listens to him speak to Brian, the more curious she becomes. She's never met anyone like Richard before and wishes she could speak with him. Instead, she simply sits on the fence and watches from afar.

"I think we may actually finish early today," says Brian as he finishes piling the rest of the waste from the stables into a wheelbarrow. "If we do, that means we can head to the bar and have ourselves a good night. Plus, we both get paid tonight, so why not celebrate?"

Richard laughs. "What are we celebrating?"

"You, making it through an entire week of work," he replies with a grin. "Not many people are able to do this type of work. They come in thinking they can make some good money quickly, but that isn't the case. Taking care of a ranch is hard work, which is something I can see you understand well."

Melissa smiles as she watches them. Even though they have only known each other for a week, they instantly hit it off. They are always laughing and joking around with each other. It makes her feel like life is still going well for her family even though her body is in a coma.

"I suppose making it through a week of work is worthy of a celebration—but only if you're paying," he jokes.

Brian pretends to look offended. "Why, how dare you expect me to take you out without expecting to pay!" Even though he is trying his best to sound serious, he can't hide the smile that spreads across his face. "Anyway, I will be back in a few. Do you mind just double-checking that the horses are good for the night before we get out of here?"

"Yeah, no problem," Richard replies before looking right at Melissa.

Since she still isn't convinced he can see her, she lifts her hand and waves to him. Much to her surprise, Richard's eyes widen, and he takes a step toward her before waving back.

He waved back. Does that mean he can see me?

Melissa sits up straight and tries to say something, but Richard only looks confused as no words leave her lips. By this point, she is convinced that he is able to see her and decides she needs to prove it to herself.

Hopping down from the fence, Melissa takes a few steps forward before pointing to Richard and then to herself as if to ask if he is able to see her. Melissa was sure her heart would be racing if she was still in her own body.

Richard tilts his head slightly as he stares in her direction before nodding. "I can see you," he says.

Melissa stands there momentarily, completely dumbfounded by the fact that he responded. While she suspected he could see her, it's different now that she has confirmation. Part of her wonders if she's made a mistake by trying to interact with him, though at the same time, she is grateful that she is no longer alone. After spending an entire month alone with no one to talk to, it was nice to have some company.

She tries again to speak, but no words leave her lips. Richard takes a few steps closer to her, looking nervous. "I can't hear what you're saying, but I would love to talk to you. Are you Melissa?"

She jolts in surprise as her name falls from his lips. Still unable to speak to him, she simply nods.

Richard frowns. "I'm sorry about what happened to you. If it makes you feel any better, I've been taking good care of your horse. He is a good steed, and I'm sure he's looking forward to you making a full recovery."

Melissa smiles even wider. Even though her parents come to visit her in the hospital sometimes, she is worried they don't believe she will pull through. Being unable to say anything to them while they grieve is one of the hardest things she's ever experienced. She opens her mouth to try and say hello to Richard, but it doesn't seem like he can hear her. Without being able to say anything to him, she isn't sure how to communicate.

"Don't worry. It's okay if you can't talk," he says with a smile. "There are still other ways to communicate. Have you been coming here every day since your accident?"

She nods in response. While she is relieved not to spend all her time at the hospital, it also hurts to be home where no one can see or help her. Honestly, she isn't even sure why Richard can see her. It gives her hope that things might eventually work out, but also has her wondering why he's the only one who seems to see her. What makes him so different?"Well, I'm glad you still feel safe enough to come home. Dusky has missed you. He tells me every day," he chuckles.

Melissa smiles, but Brian walks up behind Richard before she can do anything. "Are you ready to get out of here?" he asks, patting him on the shoulder.

Richard nods before glancing back at Melissa. She swears he looks sad, but he quickly turns his attention back to Brian. "Sounds good to me. I've just been waiting around for you."

"Did you recheck the horses?"

"The horses are fine," Richard replies. "I take pride in raising healthy horses, you know."

Brian chuckled and mounted his horse, signaling for Richard to do the same. Melissa wished more than anything that she could use her voice to speak with him, but there was nothing more she could do. Since Brian was unable to see her, Richard would need to pretend she wasn't there.

She watches as the two men ride off, leaving her alone once more. As soon as they fade from view, Melissa finds herself already missing Richard. He seems like a good man, and she wants to get to know him. Especially since he is the one looking after Dusky while she is in her coma, and the only one who can see her. While she tries her best not to think of her coma, she constantly worries that she will never wake up. It has already been a month, and she doesn't feel any closer to recovering.

She wishes there was a way to wake herself up, but nothing she did ever worked. Just as she's about to head back to the hospital, she sees her brother Mark walk out of the house with an angry expression on his face. Every piece of her wishes she could run up and comfort him as she'd always done, but for now, all she can do is watch and knock over the occasional picture.

After watching him walk for a little while, she decided to follow behind him and see what he was up to. When she draws near, she can hear him mumbling something under his breath. It isn't hard for Melissa to see there is something wrong, but knowing there is nothing she can do to help eats away at her. For over a month, she has watched her family mourn her, and now that things are finally settling down, she often finds herself wondering if her being in a coma is a burden to the rest of the family.

Mark sits down beneath an old oak tree and pulls out a small journal. Until this point, Melissa never knew he carried a journal, and she sits beside him to see what he's writing. Normally she would never invade his privacy like this, but since he is unable to see her, she figures it's the best way for her to learn how to help her brother.

As she watches him write, a slight frown appears on her face. He is writing about her, and just like her mother, he is blaming himself for what happened. She tries to tell him none of it was his fault, but it is impossible to get the words out. No matter how hard she tries, there is no voice for her to speak. She also knows that Mark isn't able to see her, and once again, she is hit with a tidal wave of guilt. Part of her wonders if it would be best for her parents just to pull the plug, but she quickly dismisses the idea.

There are too many things she wants to do, and the thought of dying and leaving it all behind scares her. If she dies and her work is lost, she feels as though her life would have been for nothing. Melissa isn't used to winning all the time, but she also isn't used to losing. It's been rough being nothing more than a spirit who is unable to talk. Most of the time, she finds herself growing bored and is constantly trying to find new ways to entertain herself.

The fact that Richard is able to see her brings her a little hope, but after a month in a coma, she is starting to wonder if waking up is even possible. After just one month, she knew the recovery would be brutal. Melissa doesn't want to think about it but finds the thought on her mind all the time anyway. All she wants is for things to return to how they were, but something tells her that things will never be the same again.

Chapter 5: Dancing Under the Stars

When Richard returns from his ride out to the bar with Brian, he sees Melissa in the stable, talking to one of the other horses. As soon as she catches Dusky in her eye, she runs up to him, and even though she can't pet him, he neighs to let her know he can see her. *At least this guy can see me, too*, she thinks. It is comforting to know that at least her horse knows she's still around.

Richard dismounts and smiles at Melissa. "Good to see you again. I was worried you wouldn't be here when I got back," he says. "Do you want to keep me company while I work on getting this place cleaned up?"

Melissa smiles and nods, wishing there was a way for her to speak with him. Having him around makes her feel less alone, and though she's still angry about her situation, she is starting to calm down a little. *At least now I'm not completely alone,* she thinks to herself.

"Great! I need to go let Brian know; I'll be right back." He flashes her another smile before turning and making his way out of the stable.

While he is walking away, Dusky turns and tries to nuzzle Melissa.

"Sorry buddy," she says. "I don't think I can pet you right now." The horse gives her a sad look and trots in place. She thinks maybe Dusky heard her for a moment and decides to try again.

"Can you hear me?" she asks.

Dusky doesn't respond, bringing more disappointment. Being unable to communicate with anyone is starting to take a toll on her, but she knows there is nothing she can do other than keep trying to wake up from her coma. As she is lost in her thoughts, Richard steps back into the barn. "Sorry about that," he says, looking right at Dusky. "Let's get all that off you so you can relax."

He walks over to the horse and removes his saddle and harness before leading him into his stall. Once he is finished ensuring Dusky is comfortable and cleaning up the stables, his attention moves back to

Melissa. "Brian said he was heading home for the night. I still have a few things I want to get done before I head in for the night. Do you want to join me?"

Melissa nods. *I would love to,* she thinks, wishing she could say it out loud. Being unable to speak definitely makes things more difficult, but the fact that Richard doesn't seem to mind much brings her a little peace of mind.

"Great!" he replies before turning to step out of the stables. "First, I want to make sure everything is ready for the horses to go out and graze tomorrow. That way, we can clean the stalls without them being in the way. You know how horses can be." He chuckles before stepping through the gate and into the pasture.

Melissa steps through the gate behind him to see the pasture looking as beautiful as ever beneath the night sky. She can easily see that Richard takes pride in his work. Ever since he started working, she's never seen him without a smile. No matter how the day goes, he always seems to be in a good mood.

She watches him as he slips his gloves on, grabs his shovel, and wanders around the pasture, picking up any trash or droppings before throwing them into a bag so it would be fresh for the horses in the morning. Even when picking up and cleaning all the waste, he still keeps a smile on his face. As he works, he talks to Melissa and tells her all about himself. "I know you can't respond to me, but I am truly grateful to have met you. You seem like a strong woman, and I believe you can pull through."

"When I was young, I lost my mom to cancer. She was always there for me, and you remind me of her. You have the same caring eyes and smile. No matter what, that woman always knew how to cheer me up, and believe it or not, I was a pretty wild kid." He chuckles. "Working at a ranch has been my dream since I was little. I know it sounds stupid, but it makes me feel good to care for animals and do whatever else I have to get done."

Melissa smiles at him. She can see the passion in his eyes when he speaks. More than anything, she finds herself wishing she could respond to him, but no matter how often she opens her mouth to speak, nothing comes out. As frustrating as it is, Richard continues speaking to her. "I know you can't say anything back, but thank you for staying and keeping me company. It's been nice."

He finishes picking up the last of the droppings in the pasture and makes his way back toward the gate. "Thank you for allowing me the opportunity to care for your horse, by the way. He is very sweet, and I love working with him. When I was a kid, I used to love watching my father work on the ranch, especially with the horses. Eventually, he let me take over. Taking care of them used to be the highlight of my day, and I would brag to everyone in school about how I would take care of them. Back then, I thought it made me seem cooler than it really did. I always dreamed of being like my father and keeping a ranch running. This is the closest I've ever gotten to this kind of work since."

Richard pulls a phone from his pocket and sets it on the fence, using a rock to keep it propped up. He presses a few buttons, and the sweet sound of music fills the air. "Would you like to dance with me?" he asks, holding his hand out to her.

Melissa's limbs seem to gain a mind of her own as she walks right over to him and tries to hold his hand. Since she is unable to actually make contact, she just remains as close to him as possible as he begins dancing. "I've never been a good dancer, either," he admits as he nearly stumbles a few times. "Would you believe there was a time in my life when I took dancing lessons? I was never very good at it, but I was determined to get it right. It took me three years of classes to figure out that it wasn't what I was meant to do with my life."

The more she listens to him, the more she starts enjoying being around him. He isn't like any of the other men she's met before, and the fact that he is still doing his best to get to know her even though she can't speak is nothing less than shocking. Everything about him makes her heart flutter. Even without her physical body, she can still feel the effect of his presence.

Part of her wishes she would just wake up so they could speak, but at the same time, she isn't so sure she wants to go back to how things were before. After everything, Melissa wants to find a place where she can settle down and start a family. It's something she's wanted for a long time, though she was never in a good enough relationship to actually consider it. She loves the ranch, but she also wishes to branch out on her own someday.

As she snaps back to reality, she realizes Richard is still dancing with her. She wishes she could speak to him and tell him how much she enjoys his company, but for now, she figures she can settle for this.

Nearly an hour goes by before Richard slowly pulls away from her in a way that makes it seem like he's forcing himself to. "I hate to say this, but I need to go turn in for the night. It will be an early morning for me, so I need to get some rest. That being said, I hope we can see more of each other tomorrow." He smiles at her before gathering his things. "I hope you have a good night," he says before tipping his cowboy hat and making his way toward his car.

Melissa watches him closely as he walks away, and though part of her wants to follow behind, she knows better. If anything, she needs some time to clear her head. She makes her way back to the hospital and is surprised to see Richard sitting there with her body. His hand is wrapped around hers, and she sees tears glistening in his eyes as he looks down at her. "I'm sorry this happened to you," he says. "Even though we've never truly met, I know you're a wonderful person."

Feeling more nervous than she has in a long time, Melissa sits down on the chair on the other side of the bed. Richard looks up after a moment to see her sitting there and smiles as he wipes away his tears. "When you wake up, I would love it if you would go to dinner with me," he says, his grin turning sheepish.

Does he want to go to dinner with me? Melissa wonders.

The thought makes her head spin, and though she loves the idea, she isn't sure she is ready for another relationship. She's never felt this way about anyone before, especially in such a short time, and she's scared that if she decides to let herself fall for him just to have her heart broken, she might never be able to pick herself back up.

Both of them sit there for a while in silence before Richard finally pulls himself to his feet and gently kisses her body's forehead, even though she can't feel it. "I look forward to the day when I get to hear your voice," he says before taking one last look at her spirit as he walks out of the room.

As soon as he is out of sight, Melissa feels like someone dropped a rock on her chest. She wishes there was more she could say or do. However, before she can put much more thought into it, the monitors attached to her body begin beeping. Melissa barely even has time to process what is happening before the room is filled with doctors and nurses.

They all surround her as her heart rate begins to increase. Within a matter of seconds, Melissa feels herself being pulled toward her body. It's a strange sensation that almost makes her feel as though she is trapped under the water. While she can hear the nurses talking to each other, she has no idea what they're saying. Fear starts to take over as she gets closer to her body.

Is this how I'm going to die? She wonders. *I don't want to die. There are so many things I want to do with my life. What happens to my family if I die? Will they be okay without me?*

Panic rises as her inner voice attacks her and threatens to pull her under. As she moves closer to her body, she can feel the pain rattling her bones and pounding in her head. Every inch of her feels like it's on fire, likely from laying so still for so long. Part of her doesn't want to be reunited with her body because she is worried that once she is, death will find her and steal her away.

The thought of dying has never scared her before, but now that she's this close to it, she's starting to wonder if maybe she should be nervous. She even tries pulling back against the forces that drag her toward her body, but nothing seems to work. Melissa has no idea what's going to happen, but she has a feeling that it's not going to be pleasant.

She doesn't even have the chance to change her mind before she feels her spirit slip back inside her body, melding them back into one. For a moment her breath is taken away, and she feels like she's drowning. Melissa tries to draw in a breath of air but is met with nothing but pain. It takes her a few moments to calm herself and her eyes slowly begin to flutter open.

Noticing all the nurses scrambling around her made her feel nervous and like something is wrong. She tries to speak, but finds herself at a loss for words as the nurses continue to look her over and monitor her vitals.

Melissa knows that since she is back in her body, this is her chance to finally meet Richard face-to-face. Even with the nurses telling her she has a long way to recovery, a mix of nerves and excitement pulse through her. She barely feels any pain as the nurses work and once they are finished checking her over, they begin asking questions. Melissa answers them the best she can until eventually falling asleep after taking some medicine.

Chapter 6: Ghost

By the time Melissa opens her eyes, she finds herself lying in the hospital bed, her soul reunited with her body. While she is relieved, her body aches from being still for so long. She tries to sit up, but a firm grip on her shoulder holds her back. Frowning, she glances beside the bed to see her brother Mark standing there. His eyes are red and puffy, and she assumes he'd been crying, but she knows he'll never admit it.

"W-what happened?" she asks, her voice quiet and scratchy from the dryness in her throat.

Mark smiles. "You were in a coma. When you went out for your ride with Dusky, he was spooked by a snake and knocked you off. It's been a little over a month. The doctors said they still want to keep you here to monitor you for a day or two, but then you'll be free to go home."

"Really?" she squealed.

He nods. "But you have to pass your physical therapy assessment first. They said if you don't pass, they may need to send you to a rehab facility until you can move on your own again without issue."

"Do they think I won't be able to move?" She tries again to sit up, only to realize Mark is still gripping her shoulder.

"Not right away," he answers sympathetically. "But you're tough, and I know you'll be back home in no time."

Melissa smiles. Even though she just woke up from her coma, her eyes are already starting to grow heavy, and within minutes, she slips back to sleep.

***

When Melissa wakes up, she realizes the sun is already beginning to set. Mark no longer stands beside her, and she assumes he has gone home for the day. She turns her head to try and call for a nurse when she sees

Richard standing on the other side of her, his eyes wide. "You're awake," he says, seemingly unable to take his eyes off her.

She nods. "What are you doing here?"

He smiles. "I was told you woke up, so I had to come see you. It's good to really see you and not just your ghost." He reaches over and gives her hand a light squeeze.

"It's good to finally be able to talk to you," she replies, feeling heat rise to her cheeks as she speaks.

"I should probably let you get some rest." He leans down and kisses her forehead gently. "Once you're feeling better, I would love to get to know you more. Now that you can talk again, I'm sure you have lots of great stories to tell me."

Melissa laughs, her chest sore from the sudden movement. "I would be happy to tell you all my stories once I'm out of this place."

"It's a deal then." He kisses her hand before letting it go and heading out of the room. As Melissa watches him walk away, she feels a flutter in her heart and wishes he would come back and stay the night.

***

It takes Melissa a little longer than expected to get back to walking again. What she believed would only take a few days dragged over a month. The recovery from her coma was awful. Her entire body burned whenever she moved, and learning to walk on her own again took a lot of work.

Eventually, she managed to work the stiffness from her joints and loosen her muscles enough that she started to feel like her old self again. By the time she finally returned home, she felt like a brand new woman. Even with all the recovery, Melissa still found ways to remain positive.

Richard came to visit her every day while she was healing, which helped, and she found herself growing closer to him the more time they spent together. When he wasn't around, she found herself missing him, and time seemed to inch by like it was molasses dripping off a spoon.

However, when he was around, time always seemed to fly right on by, and neither of them was ever without a smile on their face.

"It's good to have you back home, sis," Mark says as she steps into the kitchen to make herself a cup of coffee. It's the morning after her first night home, and Mark is sitting at the table reading through one of the checklists he had made up for the ranch.

"It's good to be home. I don't know how much longer I could have kept going to physical therapy. I admit it helped, but it was also one of the most painful experiences of my life." When the coffee is finished, she pours herself a glass before sitting down across from Mark. "What are you looking at?" she asks, gesturing to the lists in front of him.

"Just trying to figure out what we need. I plan on heading down to the store today to pick up a few things. You can come with me if you'd like."

Melissa tilts her head in surprise. "You would take me with you? I thought you hated taking me places."

"Usually, I do. And don't play coy with me. You know I don't take you places because you act like a child. You always want me to spend extra money on you too. I was hoping to save all that for when I eventually have kids."

Laughter bursts from her throat before she can stop it. "Sorry, but the thought of you having kids just doesn't seem all that feasible. I don't think I've ever even seen you speak to a kid."

"Just because I've never spoken to a kid doesn't mean I don't eventually want one of my own."

"If you say so, but I won't believe it until I see it."

"Is that a challenge?"

"It could be."

The two of them erupt with laughter right as Richard walks in with a confused expression painted across his face. "What are you doing?" he asks, unsure what to make of the situation.

"Just talking about all the kids Mark is planning to have once he finally gets a girlfriend," Melissa replies between giggles.

Richard looks at Mark, whose face is now bright red with embarrassment. "If you need a girlfriend, you know I would be happy to be your wingman," he replies with a chuckle. "And if you can't find a girl, there is always adoption!"

This sent Melissa into hysterics. She'd never even considered the thought of her brother having a child. He always seems so rough and rugged from working on the ranch, so it's hard for her to see him caring for a baby. "There you go," she says, playfully patting Mark on the shoulder. "If you choose to adopt, you don't even need to wait for a wife."

Mark shakes his head, though Melissa can see the hint of a smile dance across his face. "I don't plan on adopting any children. I'm going to find the perfect woman, and we will live happily ever after."

"That sounds more like a fairytale you just made up," Melissa replies.

"Hey, just so you know, I have a date tonight, so maybe this woman will be my future wife."

"Thinking of marriage on the first date?" Richard chimes in with a cheesy grin.

Mark stood up from the table after finishing his coffee. "Hey, don't judge me. Sometimes people just fall in love, and everything works out." He laughs before placing his dishes in the sink and heading toward the door. "Anyway, I'm going to head to the store. Let me know if you need anything."

Melissa watches her brother walk out of the room before glancing over at Richard, who is now sitting in the seat beside her. "What do you have going on today?" she asks him.

He shakes his head. "Not much. I just need to take care of the horses, and that's it. I think Mark is in charge of the rest. If you aren't sure, you could always ask your old man."

She smiles at him. "I suppose I could do that. Though ever since I've gotten home, he wants nothing more than to treat me like a fragile flower."

"You are a fragile flower," he replies with a laugh. "You're getting stronger, but I can understand why he wants to keep you safe, especially since no one knew whether or not you would wake up."

"Did you think I wasn't going to wake up?"

He shakes his head. "No. That's why I went to visit you and prayed for you every night. I'm grateful that I was able to meet you and help you through this."

"I've never experienced anything like that before. Being able to see and hear everything–including my old body–definitely didn't make me feel better. There was a time when even *I* believed that I would never wake up." She stops staring off into the distance as she reminisces and turns to meet Richard's eyes. "Honestly, I think it was your voice that woke me up. Before you started visiting me, I felt completely hopeless, but you restored that hope for me."

He smiles as he takes her hand in his. "I always believed that you would wake up, and if I truly am the one who woke you up, then you're welcome." He pushes a small strand of hair behind her ear and grins. "You know, we could always try dancing again now that you're better. If you want, we could even go out for dinner. I know this place—"

Melissa interrupts him before he can finish. "That sounds an awful lot like a date," she says, suddenly feeling nervous. While she likes Richard, she is worried about what will happen if things don't work out. Even though she wants to give him the benefit of the doubt, she's been hurt too many times by too many people. Trust is something she has a hard time coming to terms with.

Richard smiles and lifts her chin gently so he can stare into her eyes. "If you don't want it to be a date, it doesn't need to be. I would still like to take you around town."

The smile falls from her face as she stares into his eyes. More than anything, she wants to tell him never mind and simply avoid the subject, but she knows she can't. She slowly pulls her face away from his hand and stares down at her lap. "I just don't think dating would be the best idea for me right now. I'm still trying to recover, and after my last breakup, I'm not sure my heart can handle much more."

"You shouldn't have to deal with this alone. You've been through a lot and have absolutely nothing to be ashamed of. I will always be here when you need me, but I know you can take care of yourself. What happened to the beautiful and brave ghost girl I was dancing with the other day?"

Nervous jitters take over her fingers as she struggles to find a response. Even though they spent hours together before she woke up, she still feels as though seeing him in person and being able to reach out and touch him is strange. Since the moment she met him, she wanted nothing more than to hold him close, but it had been impossible. Now that it isn't, she wonders just how different things will be between them. As far as she can tell, he still looks at her with love in his eyes. "I don't know. I think I'm still just trying to find myself, and until I get that figured out, I don't think dating anyone would be a good idea."

Rejecting him isn't easy, but she knows she needs to take care of herself before trying to take on more responsibility. "I'm sorry. I—"

"You have nothing to apologize for. I'm not going anywhere, and if you don't want to date right now, then you don't have to. I've been waiting all my life for love to show up. Now that I've found you, I will wait for you forever."

Chapter 7: Family Breakfast

After a long night of tossing and turning, Melissa finally pulls herself out of bed and slips into her clothes for the day. Checking herself in the mirror, she fixes her shirt and walks to the window. It's still dark outside, so at least she didn't oversleep.

Making her way downstairs, she fills her thermos with coffee and heads out to the barn. To her surprise, Richard and Brian are already caring for their horses. "You two are up early," she says as she sets down her things. "Here I was thinking that *I* got up early. What time did you get in here?" As she looks around the barn, she knows they had to have been down there for at least an hour. It was spotless, which definitely would have taken some time.

"I was out here around three," replies Brian with a chuckle. "After taking a day off, I felt the need to jump back in as soon as possible. You know I hate being away from this place."

Melissa laughs. As long as she'd known Brian, he would always come into work early and argue with her father about how he didn't need rest and could keep working. Brian has been around for as long as she could remember, and he's always been a good family friend. "I should have guessed that you would be back this early. I know you can never stay away."

Richard chuckles. "I got here around four. Honestly, I was surprised to see Brian here already. I knew he would be back today, but finding him in the barn when it was still dark outside nearly gave me a heart attack. After having a good laugh about it, we decided to use our extra time to get the stables nice and clean because they needed it. The horses should be happier now too."

Smiling, Melissa walks over to Dusky, who begins whinnying and trotting in place when he sees her. After being in a coma for a month, she has difficulty keeping Dusky away from her. If it was possible for him to follow, he was always right behind her. He'd even jumped out of the pasture one day just to try and say hello.

As she gently stroked the horse's snout, she noticed he was already brushed and ready for the day. Melissa's attention immediately shifted to Richard, who was standing there with a sheepish smile. "I couldn't help myself. I got used to caring for him when you weren't here. I was excited to see him this morning, so I figured I would prepare him for the day to surprise you. Maybe later, we can all go out for a ride."

The mention of going out for a ride makes her legs quiver. While Melissa loves Dusky, she isn't yet ready to go out riding again. "I, uh, I think I will just stay behind. You can take Dusky out if you want. I'm just not feeling up to it."

Riding her horse used to be one of her favorite parts of her day, but now things are different. She doesn't want to risk another accident and knows that if she somehow slips into another coma, there is a good chance she will never wake up. Her chest tightens at the thought.

It isn't until she feels Richard's grip on her shoulder that she realizes she has been standing there, lost in her thoughts. "Are you okay?" he asks, his eyes filled with concern.

Melissa nods. "Yeah, I just feel a bit nervous about getting back up on Dusky. I don't want to be thrown off again."

Richard squeezes her shoulder and smiles. "It's okay. You don't have to do anything you don't want to. You can just stay here and relax all day, and that would be perfectly fine too."

Brian walks over and smiles at her. "We all have bad days. Accidents happen all the time, and everyone recovers at their own pace. Take all the time you need. By the time you get back to work, everything will just fall into place. You have every reason to be nervous, and there is no shame in it. These things happen to the best of us. We are just grateful that you're okay."

Melissa smiles as the two men try to encourage her to feel better. Being too afraid to ride Dusky makes her feel guilty, but she knows trying to ride him when she isn't up to it will only make things more dangerous.

She helps the men finish with the stable and smiles as they mount their horses and ride off toward the hills. As they fade from her sight, Melissa heads inside to grab herself a little snack. To her surprise, her father sits at the table between Mark and her Mother. "Uh, what's going on?" she asks, completely caught off guard by all of them. It's rare to see them all in one place since they're all busy around the ranch most days.

"We are just glad to have you home," Mark says, tapping a pen on the table across from her.

"Is there something going wrong?

Mark shakes his head. "No, Mom just thought it would be nice to share a meal together. What we didn't expect was for you to be so late."

Melissa frowns. "How would I be on time if I didn't know this was happening?"

"Don't worry about it," her mother says as she pulls a chair out. "I just want to have breakfast as a family like we used to. I miss having the chance to talk to you. When you were in your coma, I was worried beyond belief."

"I know, Mom," Melissa responds as she takes her seat. "It wasn't great for me either. I don't think I will be riding for a while."

"That's understandable," her dad says before shoving a forkful of eggs into his mouth.

Mark shoots a glare at his father. "It isn't understandable," he replies, shaking his head. His eyes shift toward Melissa. "You need to get back on the horse. Isn't that the saying? Well, in this case, you need to literally get back on your horse. You can't let the fear of what happened rule over your life."

"I'm not. I just don't think I'm ready to ride yet. It's scary. Every time I think about it, I just see myself being launched into the air."

"It's normal to be nervous," her mother says. "But your brother is right. Sooner or later, you're going to need to get back on the horse. You've always loved riding horses, and you can't allow one tragedy to take it away from you. I know I raised you better than that. If you need some time, I understand, but eventually, you're going to have to move forward."

Melissa isn't sure how to feel about the words she's hearing. While one part of her mind believes they are right, another part of her is worried about being hurt again. She finally begins to feel like she is getting her life back, though she also feels like a piece of her is missing—the piece of her that loves to ride.

When she doesn't respond, her dad chimes in. "Sweetheart, it's understandable that you're scared. You have every right to be. But you shouldn't let that fear control you. Tell me, do you blame Dusky for what happened?"

Her eyes widen. "What? Of course I don't blame Dusky. He was scared and reacted on instinct. If anything, it was my fault. I didn't notice the snake, and I didn't really try to calm him down either. I was just too shocked to do much. I would never blame Dusky for what happened."

"Okay," he replies. "Then why punish him because of your fears? That horse loves you, and while he has been content with Richard caring for him, he knows he belongs with you."

Melissa takes a few bites of her food and carefully thinks about their words. It's true that she doesn't blame Dusky for what happened, and she doesn't want him to feel like she's punishing him by refusing to ride him after the accident. "I will try again."

"Well, better get on it," says Mark. "The longer you wait, the harder it will be. You can't let the bad things in life hold you back from doing the things you love." He pushed away from the table and gathered his dishes to take them into the kitchen. "Anyway, I need to get going. I have a lot to get done today. Just think about what I said, okay?" He smiles at

Melissa and waves goodbye to his parents before heading out the front door.

Melissa shifts her attention to her parents, who are now gathering the rest of the dishes. "If you need help with the dishes—"

"Don't worry about the dishes," her mom cuts in. "I will take care of it. You go spend time with the animals. Get yourself reacquainted with the ranch. Make sure you're not overworking yourself."

"If you need help with anything, just come get me," her father says as he throws on his jacket. "I'll be out in the pasture most of the day. I need to pick up the new horse today and work on getting him adjusted."

"We're getting a new horse?" Melissa questions.

He nods. "I thought your brother would have told you. We are getting three more of them. They are young, so we will need to train them, but I figure it would be nice to have a few extra horses around the ranch. We have a few chicks coming next week, too, if you want to find a place for them to go."

"He didn't tell me, but I look forward to meeting them later. I'll stop by this afternoon to see if there's anything I can do to help." Melissa kisses both her parents goodbye and makes her way out of the house. Looking over at the stables, she sees Richard walking out, leading Dusky toward the pasture.

Wasting no time, she walks over to him and smiles. "How was your ride?"

A bright smile spreads across his face as Richard turns his head to look at her. "It was good. Though I think it would have been even better if you were there."

Heat rises to her cheeks, and she quickly looks down at the ground, not wanting him to see her reddened skin. "Maybe one of these days we can ride together," She says, her voice nearly a whisper.

"I would like that," He says as they reach the pasture. He opens the gate to let Dusky through and turns all his attention toward Melissa.

"How are you feeling, by the way? I know you are still recovering, but you seem to feel better."

She nods. "I'm actually feeling much better. It's been rough, but I finally feel like I'm getting back to my old self." Melissa looks over at Dusky as he trots around the pasture before finding a comfortable spot in the shade to graze. "I am nervous about trying to ride again, though."

Richard smiles. "You have nothing to worry about. If you want to ride again, I will be right there to help you. If you need support, then I'm your man."

Melissa can't help but crack a smile. The more time she spends with Richard, the stronger her feelings for him grow. Part of her wishes they could be together, but another part of her still isn't sure if she's ready for such a big commitment. "Thank you. Maybe tomorrow we can try," She says, finally looking back at him.

"Tomorrow sounds perfect." Richard's smile widens as she nods in agreement.

Even though neither of them say anything for the next few minutes, Melissa finds herself at peace. Being around Richard is always comforting, especially since he is the only person that knows what she went through while in her coma. The fact that he stuck around even after she woke up said a lot about him to her, and she wanted to get to know him better now that they had a chance to finally communicate.

Chapter 8: New Adventures

A few weeks pass by before Melissa finally finds herself able to get back on her horse. The first few tries were brutal—she couldn't even get herself in the saddle—but now that she's gained back some of her confidence, she is proud to be riding Dusky. She tells him how sorry she is for not riding him for so long. It feels great for her to be back on the horse, though she still has a long way to go before she'll be able to ride as fearlessly as she used to.

She spent nearly every day with Richard, and the connection between them grew stronger. One night after finishing with all their chores for the day, Richard reaches for her hand as she turns to walk away and asks her if she would like to spend a little time with him before she heads inside.

When she agrees, he leads her out to the pasture and pulls her into his arms. The stars glow brightly above them as he begins to hum a tune and dance with her. "Remember when we danced before?" he asks as he leads the dance. "It's different now that I can hold you properly."

Even without music, Melissa finds herself melting in his arms as she flows around the pasture with him. Being able to dance with him for real is like nothing she could have expected, and she finds herself wishing the moment would last forever. "It's nice," she replies softly. "The first time we danced was the only time I felt happy after my accident. I honestly wasn't sure if I was going to die or not. I was scared and alone, but you gave me something to hold onto. You gave me a reason to fight."

Richard pulls her closer as he slows down the dance. "I'm glad I did. You're a strong woman, Melissa," he says as his eyes lock with hers.

Their faces are only inches apart, and Melissa feels her heart racing. She wants him to kiss her, though she is also nervous about letting herself get too close. Right as she opens her mouth to say something, Richard speaks up again. "Melissa, would you do me the honor of having dinner with me?" he asks, his tone calm and even.

Even though she isn't sure she's ready, she can't bring herself to say no. Not when Richard has already done so much to help her. "I would love to go to dinner with you," she nearly whispers in response. "Just tell me when and where, and I'll make sure I'm ready."

A wide grin spreads across his face. "What about now? And we can go wherever you want."

Surprised by how spontaneous his request is, Melissa can't help but giggle. "It's nearly midnight, and you want to go get food?"

He nods. "I do. If you want to, that is."

"You know what? Why not, let's go." Melissa has never done anything like this before in her life, but something about Richard draws her in. Even though she isn't sure she's ready to open herself up to a relationship, she can't help but admit that her feelings for Richard grow stronger every day. The more time they spend together, the more she wants to be with him. Whenever they're together, she feels like her life is slowly falling into place.

Within half an hour, they are already in the car and on their way to the nearest 24-hour restaurant. "This is a place I used to love coming to with my parents," he says as he parks his black and blue truck in the parking lot. "Trust me; you won't be disappointed."

He walks over to her side and opens the door for her so he can help her down. When they walk into the restaurant, the place seems quiet, and there are only a few tables with people at them. "This is really peaceful at night, isn't it?" She asks with a shy giggle.

Richard nods. "It is. I'll admit it isn't the most romantic or prettiest looking place ever, but the food is to die for."

One of the waitresses walks over to them before Melissa can respond. "Welcome," she says with a smile. "You can take a seat wherever you'd like, and I will bring your menus to you and take your drink orders."

Both of them smile at the waitress and thank her before heading to one of the tables by the window. While it was easy to tell the place is old, everything inside is perfectly clean. Even the old pictures on the walls were clean and free of dust. "I can tell that whoever owns this place really cares about it," she mutters as she looks around.

"The owner does love this place," Richard responds. "I met them once or twice. It used to be run by this old man and his wife. Unfortunately, his wife passed away a few years ago, but he's kept this place up and running since, so he had to have done something right."

The waitress sets their menus down on the table and pulls out her notepad and pen. "Is there anything I can get you both to drink?"

"I'll just take some water," Melissa replies.

"Water sounds good for me, too," Richard says.

The waitress smiles at them and nods before taking off to get their water. Melissa's eyes shift back to Richard. "Thank you for bringing me here. I'm having a lot of fun."

He chuckles. "We haven't even gotten our food yet."

Melissa smiles. "That's okay. I just like being around you. You're the first person to ever truly see me. It's beautiful and terrifying all at the same time."

"Why terrifying?"

"Because it's unfamiliar. If I'm being honest, I've never felt like this before."

He grins. "I suppose that makes sense." His expression softens and he reaches across the table to take both her hands in his as he says, "Melissa, I've been falling for you since the moment we met. I may not have been able to hold you or touch you like I am now, but from the second I laid eyes on you, I started falling in love. You're the only woman I ever need, but if you still need time to figure things out, I am more than happy to give you your space."

His response wasn't what she expected, and when he says he is falling in love with her, she feels her heart flutter. More than anything, she aches to tell him she feels the same. To tell him that she loves spending time with him. But she couldn't. After everything she's been through, she isn't sure she will ever be ready for a serious relationship.

It would be a commitment, and it would mean opening up her heart. Something she has been hesitant to do since the brutal end of her last relationship. Neither of them had been ready, and when they broke up, she remembers sitting on the front porch of the house and crying for hours. She had just started to recover before she had the accident.

Pushing the thoughts from her mind, she returns her attention to Richard and smiles as she gently squeezes his hands. "I feel it is important for me to be honest here," she says, trying to sort through the clutter in her mind. "My feelings for you are strong. Stronger than they've ever been for anyone. But I don't think now is the best time for me to think about these things. There is still so much I need to take care of, and—"

Before she can finish speaking, she feels Richard's thumb swipe the space below her eye, removing the tear she was trying to hide. "You don't need to explain yourself, Melissa. Whenever you're ready, I will be here. Even if you're never ready, you will always have me as a friend."

Melissa smiles, and the rest of their dinner goes by in the blink of an eye. They talk about everything they can think of. Melissa tells him stories of her past and how she used to run around the ranch with her brother when they were younger. Richard told her all about what it was like for him growing up. His parents used to have a ranch, but even though they sold it when they were older, Richard never got tired of ranch life.

He explains how much his job means to him and how much he loves her family. They laugh and eat, and before they know it, Richard is already driving her home. Melissa is sad that the night is over. "This was one of the best nights I've had in a very long time," she says as they pull into the ranch.

Richard smiles as he parks the car in the driveway. "I'm glad to hear that," he says as he leans a little closer, his eyes locking with hers. "This may be out of line, but I would like to kiss you—only if you're okay with it of course."

Melissa can tell how nervous he is, and giggles as she nods. "How can I say no?" she says, unable to reject the request. She's been thinking of kissing him since the moment they met.

At the confirmation of her approval, Richard closes the space between them and gently presses his lips to hers. Melissa feels her chest explode with emotions the second they connect. It's like a million fireworks being fired off at once and is like nothing she's ever experienced before. She wonders if this is the feeling people talk about when they try to explain love.

When he pulls away, Melissa stares into his eyes and smiles. "Thank you for a wonderful night."

He chuckles. "You have nothing to thank me for. I'm just honored that I finally got a chance to get to know you. You're an amazing woman, Melissa, and I will do whatever I can to ensure that you are happy and taken care of. Working on the ranch with your family is my dream come true."

"I'm glad. Everyone here loves you, and you fit right in."

Richard gets out of the truck so he can open the door for Melissa. "Would you like me to walk you to the door, my lady?" he asks with a grin.

Melissa snorts, unable to control her laughter. "My lady? I don't think anyone has ever said that to me before, so thank you for the interesting experience. We will need to do this again sometime." She loops her arm around his. "And I would love for you to walk me to the door, Good Sir." Melissa is barely able to contain her laughter as he walks her up to the door.

"I will see you bright and early, Melissa," he says as he reluctantly lets go of her arm.

She feels an empty space where his hand used to be and looks at him as he walks back to the truck. "Goodnight, Richard. I hope you get some good rest. We have a long day ahead of us tomorrow."

When she sees his truck pulling away, she slips into the house and closes the door before turning the bolt. Much to her surprise, Mark was sitting in the chair in the living room, still wide awake. "Are you feeling okay?" Melissa inquires as she walks over and sits down beside him. "I thought you were done for the day."

He nods. "I am done for the day, but it never hurts to get a head start. I just want to make sure all the animals are taken care of, and then I'll be on my way to take a nap."

"Do you honestly think you're going to have time to take a nap? There is a lot to do around here."

"You know I can handle it. Stop trying to act like I can't." He cracks a slight smile. "Anyway, you go get some rest."

Melissa nods and reaches her room, shutting the door behind her. As she lays in her bed, all she can think about is her night with Richard. Everything about him seems perfect to her, and she knows she won't be able to hide the intense feelings growing in her heart for much longer. She still doesn't feel ready to be with him yet, but hopes that one day she is able to work up the courage for a new adventure.

Chapter 9: Unexpected

The following morning, Melissa makes her way to the stables to find Brian standing there brushing his horse. "Where is Richard?" she asks as she walks over to Dusky.

"I just got off the phone with him," Brian replies. "He says he was in an awful lot of pain last night, so I told him to go ahead and take the day off. Of course, he refused this request, so I would assume he will be here in about twenty minutes or so." Brian finishes brushing his horse and starts cleaning its hooves. "Don't forget all the horses are going to need new shoes soon, so you may want to make sure Dusky is nice and clean before that happens."

Melissa nods. "Don't worry, I'm already way ahead of you," she says as she grabs the brush and begins grooming her horse. After everything that happened, Melissa missed caring for Dusky. It used to always be her favorite part of the day, but things felt different now.

Almost the moment she finishes grooming Dusky and cleaning his hooves, Richard stumbles into the stable. His breathing sounds labored, and his skin is pale, with a thin layer of sweat seeping down his skin. "Good morn—" he tries to say before doubling over in pain.

Wasting no time, Melissa rushes to his side. "Richard, what's wrong? Are you okay?"

He shakes his head. "I want to say yes, but that would be a lie."

She turns back toward Brian. "Call an ambulance, I think there is something seriously wrong here."

Brian nods and pulls his phone from his pocket. Melissa turns her attention back to Richard. "It's okay," she says shakily. "We are going to make sure you get help." Tears well in her eyes as she looks at him. She could see the pain that pulsed through him when he doubled over, looking as though he was ready to vomit.

Everything that happens over the next hour is a blur. After the paramedics arrive, Melissa gets into the ambulance with Richard, doing her best to comfort him in any way she could. They rushed to the hospital, and according to the nurses, his appendix is ready to burst, so he needs surgery right away.

Melissa's eyes are locked on the ground as Brian sits down beside her. "I called your parents and your brother. They said they will be here a little later to check on him."

The sound of his voice pulls Melissa from her thoughts. "Do you think he's going to be okay? You don't think he got here too late, do you?" For the first time in her life, Melissa has found someone who truly cares for her. Every moment she spends with Richard is like magic, and knowing there is a chance that it will all be ripped away before she can tell him how she feels about him breaks her heart in a way she would never be able to explain with words.

Brian shakes his head. "I think he will be fine. This is a good hospital, and Richard is a strong man."

Time feels like it's moving slower as she waits for the nurses to come back with good news. Brian's words help her calm herself, though she can't help but be scared for Richard. Eventually, her brother and parents show up. When they do, Brian says he needs to go take care of a few things and to keep him updated. Melissa's parents promise they will and sit down on either side of her. "Are you okay, sweetheart?" her mother asks.

"I don't know," Melissa replies honestly. "He has been there for me since I was—since I woke up from my coma. He made my life so much easier, and Dusky loves him. I just want him to be okay." She can't help but mentally kick herself for not agreeing to be with him before this happened. Despite her feelings, she always believed it was a bad idea, but now that there is a chance she will never see him again, she starts to realize just how fast time flies by and that she wants him more than anything.

When she had been in her coma, it felt like an eternity, but now that she was alive again, things were different. All it takes is a second, and the things you love most can be torn away in the blink of an eye. The thought brings tears to her eyes, but her mother promptly wipes them away. Her father wraps his arms around her and pulls her close.

"I know this is hard for you, but Richard is a strong man, I have no doubt in my mind that he will make it through this without any issues. This is a very common surgery. People have this happen all the time, and he will be back to normal in no time."

Melissa smiles, even though she knows he is only trying to make her feel better. Before she can open her mouth to respond to him, the nurse walks out into the hallway. "Are you all here for Richard?" she asks as she approaches them.

"Yes, is he okay?" Melissa blurts out before anyone else gets the chance to say anything.

The nurse smiles. "He is going to be okay. He is out of surgery and is resting now. You can visit him in about an hour if you'd like."

"I would love that," she says before looking over at her parents. "Are you going to stay?"

Her father shakes his head. "I wish I could, but I still have work that needs to be done on the ranch." He looks at the nurse. "Thank you so much, and please let the doctor know I am grateful to him for saving my future son-in-law."

Heat rises to Melissa's cheeks, and she instantly turns her gaze to the ground to try and hide her blushing face. He chuckles and pats her on the shoulder. "I will see you when you get home, sweetheart."

Her mother stands up beside her and gives her a hug. "If you need a ride home later, just give me a call. The only thing I need to get done today is grocery shopping, so I should be ready for you when you call."

Melissa smiles at her parents and nods as she wipes more tears from her eyes. "Thank you both for being here." She glances at her mom. "I will call you when I am ready."

She watches her parents as they walk through the door casting her attention toward the hallway she had seen Richard being taken down in a stretcher. Not being able to see what is happening is starting to drive her insane, but she does her best to at least appear calm.

It feels like an eternity for Melissa before the nurse walks back over to her. "If you would like, you may come to visit him now. He just woke up. Bear in mind that he may still feel a little groggy."

Melissa stands up and nods. "Yes, I would love to see him; thank you."

"Of course, follow me," says the nurse.

Melissa stands up and grabs her bag before following the nurse down the hallways. Eventually, they come to a room labeled "Room 40." She steps inside right after the nurse to see Richard lying there. Machines beep all around him, but he is awake. "Hey, she says as she takes a seat beside his bed. "How are you feeling?"

He smiles and reaches over to take her hand in his. "I feel great. It's a good thing I came in when I did."

The nurse interrupts before I can respond. "I need to take your blood pressure and check your vitals really quick," she says as she pulls out a blood pressure cuff and wraps it around his arm. "Try to stay still while we check so we can get the most accurate results."

While the blood pressure cuff is working, the nurse listens to his heart, checks his temperature, and brings him a pain pill. When the blood pressure cuff stops, she looks at the monitor and records the results. "Lookin good," she says as she finishes writing her notes. "I will be back to check up on you in a little bit."

And just like that, the nurse is already back out the door. Turning her attention back toward Richard, Melissa can't help but smile. She is relieved that he is okay, though she is also having some conflicting thoughts. Her feelings for him are stronger than ever, and while she is still scared to jump into a relationship, the last thing she wants to do is miss her chance.

She realizes that Richard could have died, and everything they had would be gone. Melissa wants to build more memories with him and maybe even spend her life with him. "I'm really happy you're okay," she says, wiping a tear from her cheek before he can see it. "I'm sorry this happened to you."

"Why are you sorry?" he asks with a chuckle. "If anything, this is my fault. My appendix was going to explode on me, and instead of going to the hospital, I tried my best to tough it out. However, since I didn't want to die, I figured the hospital might as well be the place to go. Though, while I'm here, I would appreciate some company."

Melissa smiles and stands up, her hand still in his. "Richard, I think I want to give us a try," she says in a barely audible whisper. Her nerves are starting to get the better of her, though she does her best to push them down deep.

His eyes widen slightly. "What do you mean by that?" he asks, though Melissa can still see the spark in his eyes.

"You know what I mean," she replies with a giggle. "Seeing you almost die made me realize that I don't want to waste the time I *do* have with you. You're unlike anyone I've ever met before, and I want to be with you."

Richard grins widely. "If that's the case, you know you're always welcome in my arms," he says as he spreads them wide to pull her into a hug.

She is careful not to touch his wound, and before she can say anything, Richard pulls her closer and presses his lips to hers. Just like before, Melissa feels fireworks going off in her chest. All her worries suddenly melt away, and she feels she is exactly where she is supposed to be. For the first time in a long time, she feels as though everything is finally falling into place.

Chapter 10: Wedding Bells

Once Richard is released from the hospital, he heads right back to work. Melissa has just finished brushing Dusky when she turns around to see Richard standing in the doorway. "Hey there, beautiful," he says before stepping inside and pulling her into his arms. It's been a little over a week since his appendicitis, and despite all Melissa's questions, he insists that he's okay to be back at work.

"Are you sure you're feeling okay?" she asks him for the hundredth time. "You shouldn't overexert yourself. I don't want you to get hurt—"

His lips connect with hers before she can finish speaking. A smile makes its way across her lips as she pulls away and stares up into his eyes. "You don't need to worry about me getting hurt, love. If I wasn't okay, I wouldn't be here." He stands up straight. "Actually, I was thinking today would be a great day for us to go for a ride. We can take the horses up to the grassy field."

Melissa nods. "I would like that. I just finished getting Dusky all cleaned up, so all I need to do now is saddle him. How about your horse? I heard you plan to ride him today."

Richard nods. "I did. He's tied up right outside. I'll meet you out there when you're done saddling up Dusky." He smiles before turning and heading back out of the stable.

Throwing the saddle over Dusky, she secures it in place and checks to make sure she has everything she needs before leading him out of the stable. Once outside, her eyes instantly shift toward Richard. She's never seen his horse before now, and she can't keep her eyes off it. "Your horse is beautiful," she says, completely awestruck. His horse whinnied at her in response. His mane was long and black, cascading down its neck, and its fur was a deep chestnut color with swirls of white and red in multiple places.

"Thank you. He's a bit old, as I've had him for a while now, but he's reliable and will always get you where you want to go."

Melissa can see the pride in his eyes when he speaks about his horse, and it brings a smile to her face. Taking a deep breath, she turns her attention toward Dusky and pats him on his neck. "I don't know how well this will go, buddy, but we're going to give it a try."

Even though it's been a while since her accident, she still finds riding hard most of the time. She finds herself constantly afraid of being thrown off, and while she wants to trust Dusky again, she knows it is something she will have to work up to over time. Before she can think about it any longer, Melissa swallows her fear and mounts her horse. Her heart pounds hard against her chest, but she ignores it as she looks back over at the handsome cowboy beside her. "Are you ready?" She asks, trying to display more confidence than she feels.

"I'm ready whenever you are," he says with a smile.

They begin their walk, heading toward the small trail that leads up to the grassy field. Melissa can hardly even remember the last time she's been up there, though she knows Dusky has been there a few times with her father and once or twice with Richard. "What made you decide you want to ride up to the grassy field?" she asks, glancing over at him.

He responds with a grin. "I just had a feeling it would be the perfect place for us to go. No one is ever up there, and I thought it would be nice to have some time with just the two of us."

"That does sound nice," she replies with a giggle. "It's been forever since I've been up here, so I suppose I'm due."

Richard laughs, and the two of them talk all the way up the path. By the time they finally reach the end of the trail, Melissa is still trying to calm herself from all the laughter. Never in her life has anyone made her laugh the way Richard does, and she knows at that moment he is the man she is supposed to be with.

Once they make it into the beautiful green field, Richard dismounts his horse and hitches it to the post beside him. Melissa does the same with Dusky and turns around to find Richard down on one knee, holding a small black box in his hands.

Melissa feels her heart skip a beat, and all she can do is stare at him as tears threaten to fall from her eyes. "Melissa Anderson, will you marry me?" He opens the box, and in the middle sits a beautiful gold and diamond ring. Everything about it is perfect, and it is all she can do to keep herself from crying.

When she finally is able to compose herself, Melissa nods, no longer able to control the tears that have filled her eyes. "Yes, I would love to marry you, Richard," she says, her voice breaking when she speaks.

Richard beams as he takes the ring and carefully places it on her finger before standing up to meet her eyes. "Melissa, I love you. I want to spend the rest of my life with you. That ring is so much more than a ring. It's a promise that no matter what life throws our way, I will always be here for you."

Once the ring is on her finger, Melissa stares at it for a moment before pulling Richard into a tight hug. "This is why you brought me here, isn't it?"

He laughs. "Of course. Where else would I take you to propose? You and I both know this ranch is your favorite place in the world."

The two of them stayed in each other's embrace for a few minutes before taking a seat on the grass. They spend most of the day talking while their horses graze in the field. Before Melissa knows it, the sun has begun to dip beneath the clouds. Richard and Melissa hold each other close as they watch the beautiful colors overtake the captivating Montana sky.

***

Even though it's only been three months since Richard proposed, Melissa is ready to move forward with the wedding. Mark and her parents help her make plans and do their best to take most of the stress off of her. Upon finding out that she and Richard were engaged, the entire family began curiously questioning her and congratulating her. "Does this mean I will have a few little grandbabies running around here soon?" Her mother asks as she walks up behind her to help fix her dress. "No pressure or anything, I just think it would be nice to have little ones around again."

Melissa laughs. "I wouldn't hold your breath. I don't plan on having kids for at least two or three years."

Her mother smiles and kisses her cheek. "I'm so very proud of you, Melissa. You've overcome so much, and I am so proud to call you my daughter. This wedding will be beautiful." She steps away from Melissa and looks her up and down. "What do you think of this one?" she asks, gesturing to the dress she is wearing.

Trying to get a better look at herself, Melissa turns and looks in the mirror. While the dress doesn't fit perfectly, she knows her mother will fix it. The dress is eggshell white with fleece on the sleeves and a sleek bottom. It isn't too tight, and out of all the dresses she's tried, she definitely finds this one to be much more comfortable. "I think this dress is perfect." She says, turning her attention back to her mother. "Will you be able to get it adjusted?"

Her mother smiles. "Of course. It won't take me too long, and it's nothing I can't handle. The only thing you need to worry about is taking care of yourself. This day is your day, and I won't let you ruin it by running around and trying to do chores."

"Have I ever told you that you're the best mom ever?"

"Yes, but I wouldn't mind hearing it more often," she replies with a laugh.

"Fair enough," Melissa says. "Anyway, I need to finish getting ready. Dad said there was something he wanted to talk to me about too."

"Sounds good. The wedding starts in a few hours, and I don't want you to be late. I also don't want you to get all dirty before the ceremony."

"Don't worry, I will be quick," she says before kissing her mother on the cheek. "I'll leave the dress with you so you can fix it up." Melissa pulls off the dress and throws on a t-shirt and some shorts before heading out of the house and to the pasture where she finds her father training one of the new horses.

"Hey, Dad," she says, trying to gain his attention. "What did you want to talk to me about?

He turns around when he hears her speak and smiles. "I know this is your day and that you're excited for your wedding. You know I will be there supporting you, but I do need to know if you want me to walk you down the aisle."

Melissa is taken aback in surprise. "Of course I want you to walk me down the aisle!" she blurts out. "You're my dad. I wouldn't have anyone else give me away but you." She can see the tears welling behind his eyes, which only causes hers to water more.

Before she can say anything, her father pulls her into a tight hug. "I love you sweetheart, and I am so proud of you and I am so happy to see you getting married to someone you truly love. Everyone here is here to support you, so if you need anything at all just let me know."

Melissa hugs him tighter. "Thank you, Dad."

After a little while, Melissa finds herself standing in the kitchen with her mom, finishing the final details of her makeup. "Are we almost done?" She questions, noticing it is starting to get close to the wedding start time.

"Just one more thing... There we go! You are ready to go," She says as she places the makeup box down beside her. Grabbing the mirror off the table, she turns it so Melissa can see how she did her hair.

Upon seeing herself, Melissa almost bursts into tears. Not that long ago, she had been in a coma, worried she would never be able to wake up. Now, she is finally starting to gain traction and is proud to be marrying her best friend.

After a few minutes, her father walks up beside her—all dressed up with a proud smile on his face. "Are you ready? Everyone is already at the top of the hill waiting for you."

Melissa takes a deep breath and nods. "Yes. I'm ready."

He smiles and takes her arm to lead her out the door. As soon as they step outside, wedding music begins playing, and she notices her parents hired a small band to play the music. Since she hadn't been allowed to help with everything during the planning stage, she has no idea what she is getting herself into.

Plenty of friends and family she hasn't seen in years are gathered around the grassy field as Melissa's father walks her down the aisle. At the end, she can see Richard standing there waiting for her. There is a wide smile on his face, and he looks like he is on the brink of tears.

Upon seeing him standing there, Melissa feels a few tears escape and run down her cheeks. Seeing him there waiting for her, she knows she finally found her soulmate. When her father makes it all the way down the aisle, he kisses his daughter on the cheek before heading to take his seat.

The ceremony that follows is beautiful and way beyond anything she expected. Both of them cry as they read their vows to each other, and by the time Richard is told to kiss the bride, he pulls her close and wraps his arms around her as the warmth of his lips presses against her own.

All the guests cheer loudly, and Melissa can't help but smile as she stares into Richard's eyes. "I have one more surprise for you," he says as he takes her hand. "Come with me."

He leads her back down the hill where they find their horses freshly groomed and waiting for them. Dusky is even wearing a bowtie and his mane has been beautifully braided. "Is this your surprise?" She asks, looking over at her new husband.

Richard smiles. "Not quite. I've rented us a vacation home for our honeymoon. It has a stable for the horses, and everything is all ready to go."

Melissa smiles and kisses him once more before mounting her horse. Once they are both ready, Melissa waves back at her family as they cheer for her. She can see her mother and father crying, and even Mark looks as though his eyes are ready to spring a leak. The sight makes Melissa happy.

She knows this is exactly where she belongs and feels so lucky that her life turned out this way.

After saying their goodbyes, Melissa and Richard exchange loving smiles and ride off into the sunset.